A CHILD'S GUIDE TO
DEATH

Written by Dustin LaValley, John Edward Lawson, and Mark Sullivan

Illustrated by Darin Malfi

RAW DOG
SCREAMING
PRESS

From Dustin:

This one is for Brandon Estes.

A special thank you is adequate to the following for their support and friendship: Ron Malfi, Darin Malfi, John Edward Lawson, Jennifer Barnes, Edward Lee, Mark Sullivan, Chris Williams, and Danny NSK.

A Child's Guide to Death © 2007
by Dustin LaValley, John Edward Lawson, Mark Sullivan, and Darin Malfi

Published by Raw Dog Screaming Press
Hyattsville, MD

First Edition

Cover and interior illustrations: Darin Malfi
Book design: M. Garrow Bourke

Printed in the United States of America

ISBN: 978-1-933293-48-6

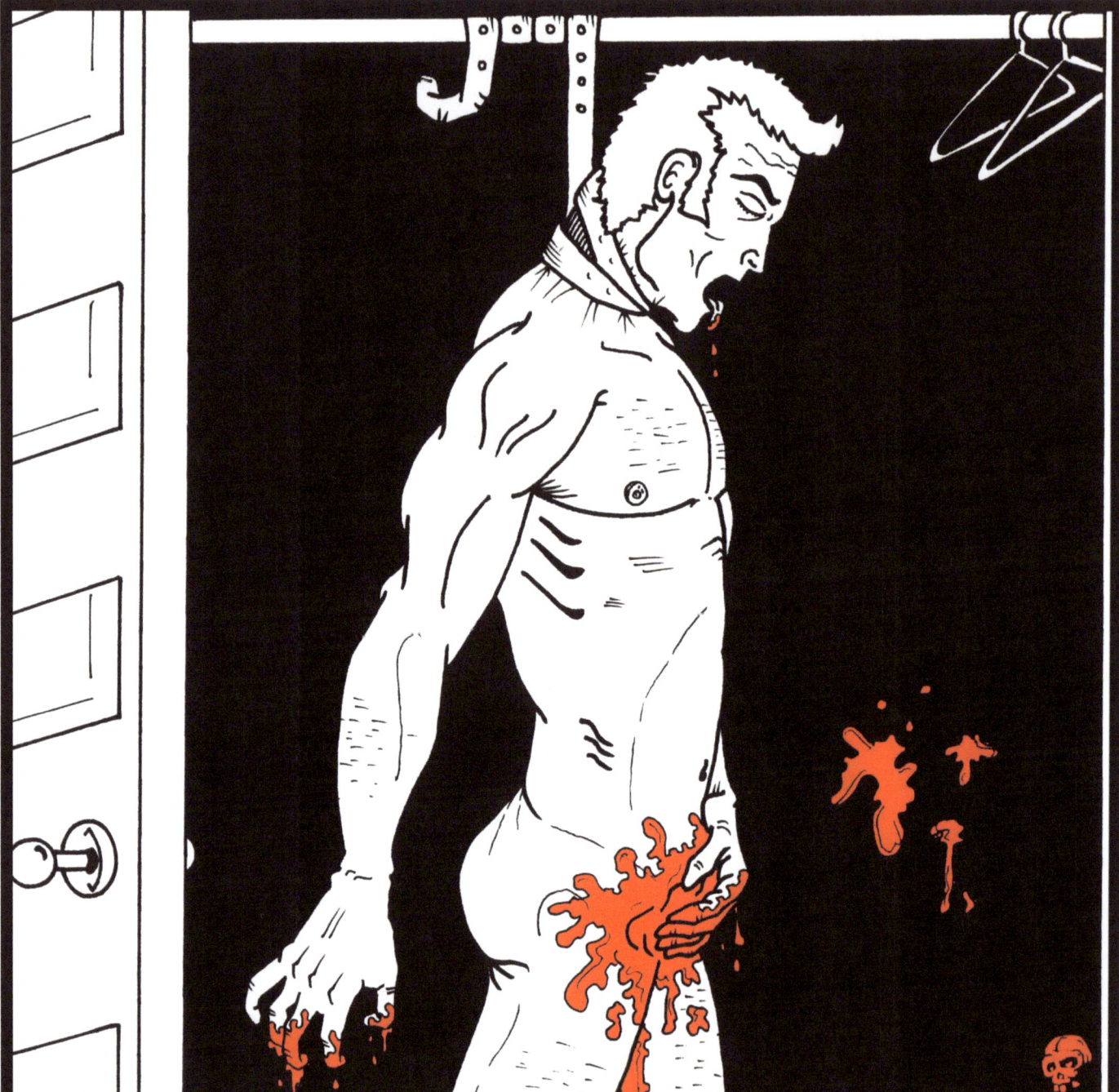

AUTO EROTIC ASPHYXIATION

It has nothing to do with your car collection or your ass fixation. It has everything to do with a lack of oxygen intensifying your orgasm even as it hinders your ability to undo the belt around your neck. It probably has something to do with your kid's mental condition after discovering your bloated corpse.

BEAR ATTACK

Even when riding unicycles with little red hats atop their heads, these real life plush novelties will not hesitate to steal your picnic basket and tear out your jugular.

CRUCIFIXION

There's something phallic about a spike penetrating flesh, something deadly about being nailed to beams of wood...and there's definitely something disturbing about wearing an instrument of torture around your neck.

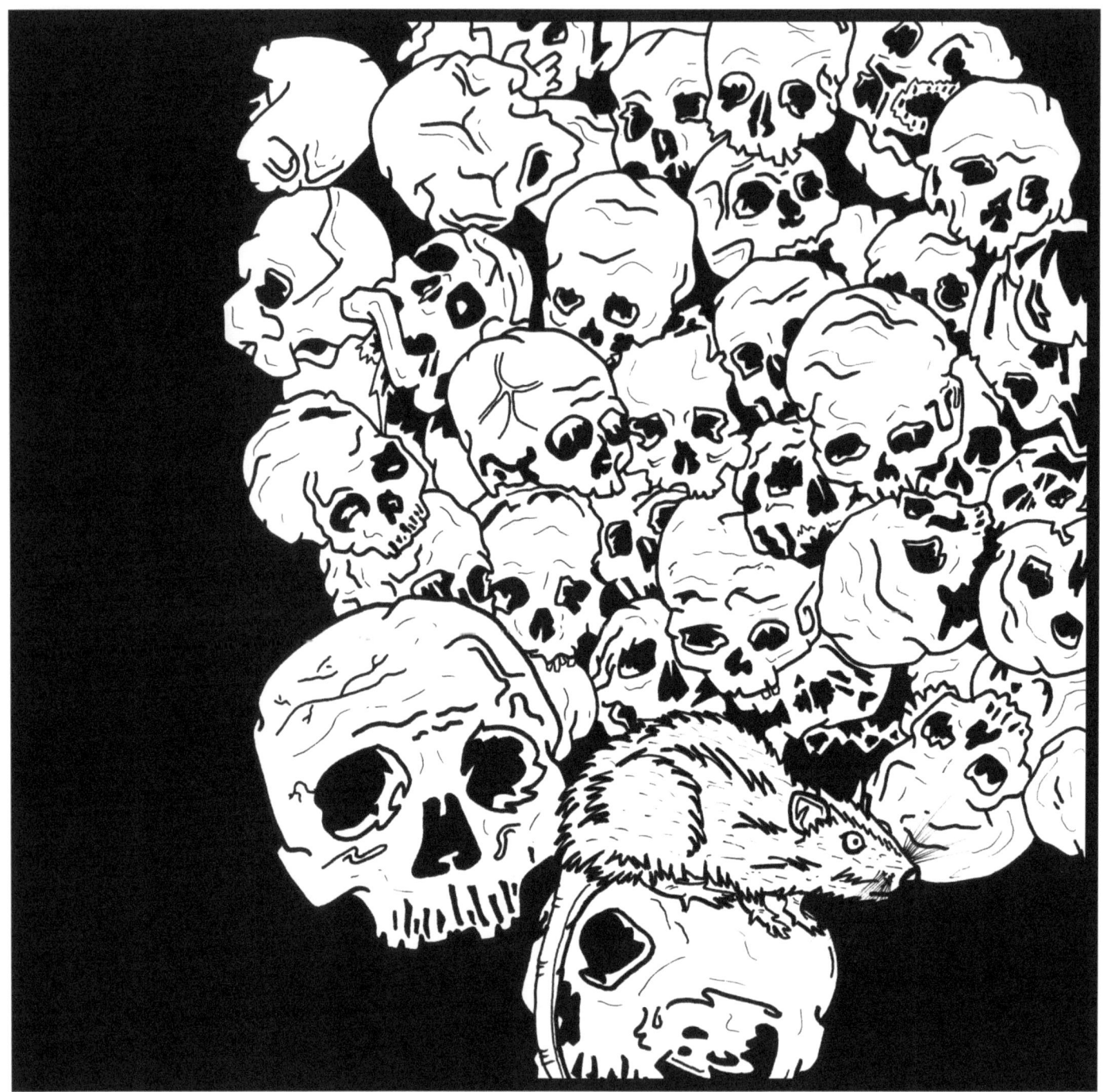

DECOMPOSITION

Six-feet-deep, dry and tight, your skin will wither and crack and tear. Six-feet-deep, dark and cold, your senses will drown in the putrid and the rotten and the horrid realization of consciousness reborn.

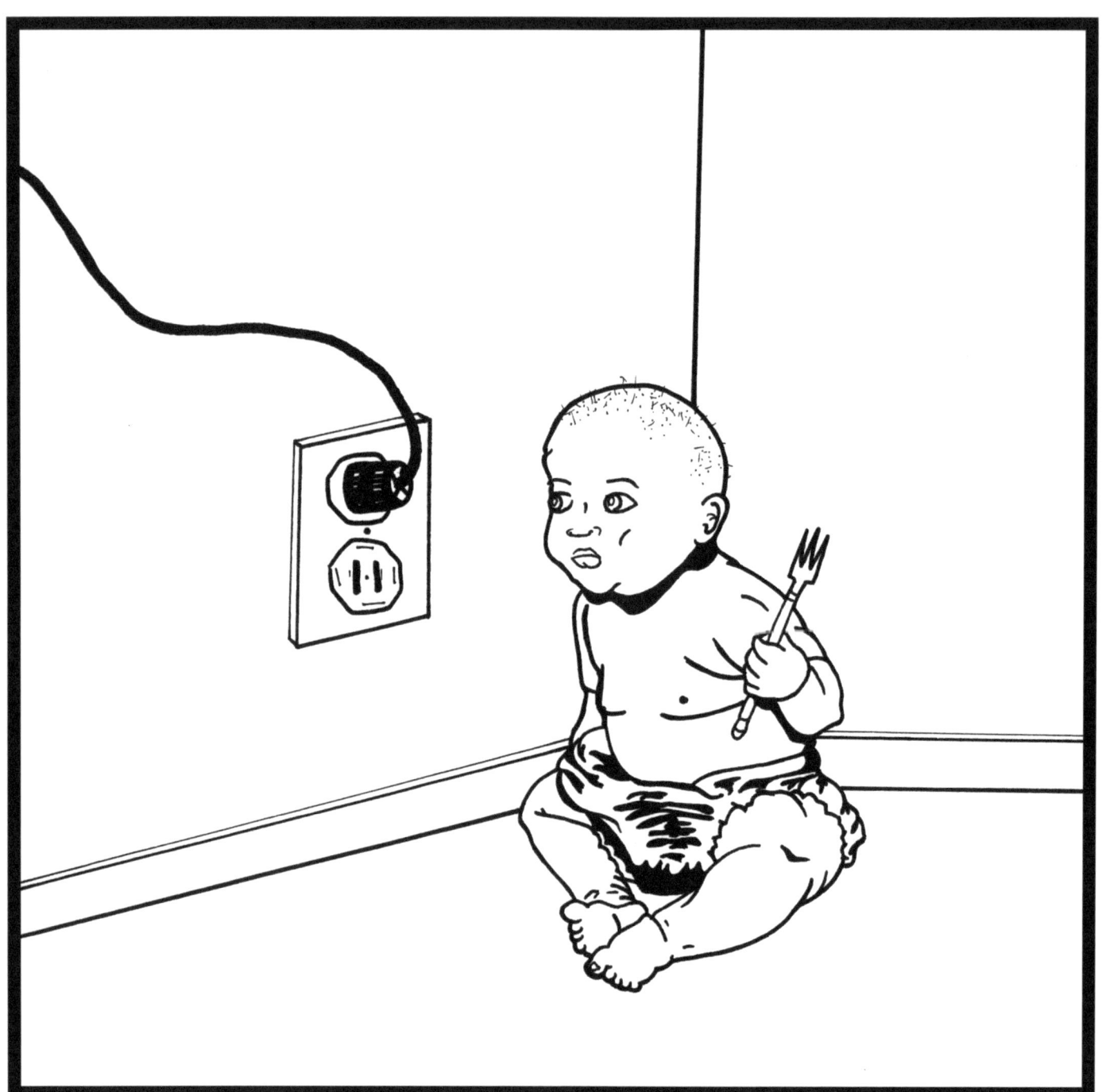

ELECTROCUTION

Officially, electric current is good for Muslim genitals and violent criminals; bad for toddlers exploring sockets and electricians with poor eyesight.

FIREWORKS

If the Declaration of Independence stands for anything, it's our freedom to celebrate the nation's birth drunk with explosives smoking in mangled hands.

GANG BANGERS

10,000 Mother Fuckers sounds like a great porno idea before you try it, but things tend to get messy after the first 3,000 guys, give or take a few hundred.

HUNTING MISHAP

Fat, drunken rednecks with guns... An accident waiting to happen, or, would it more likely be stated: waiting for an accident to happen?

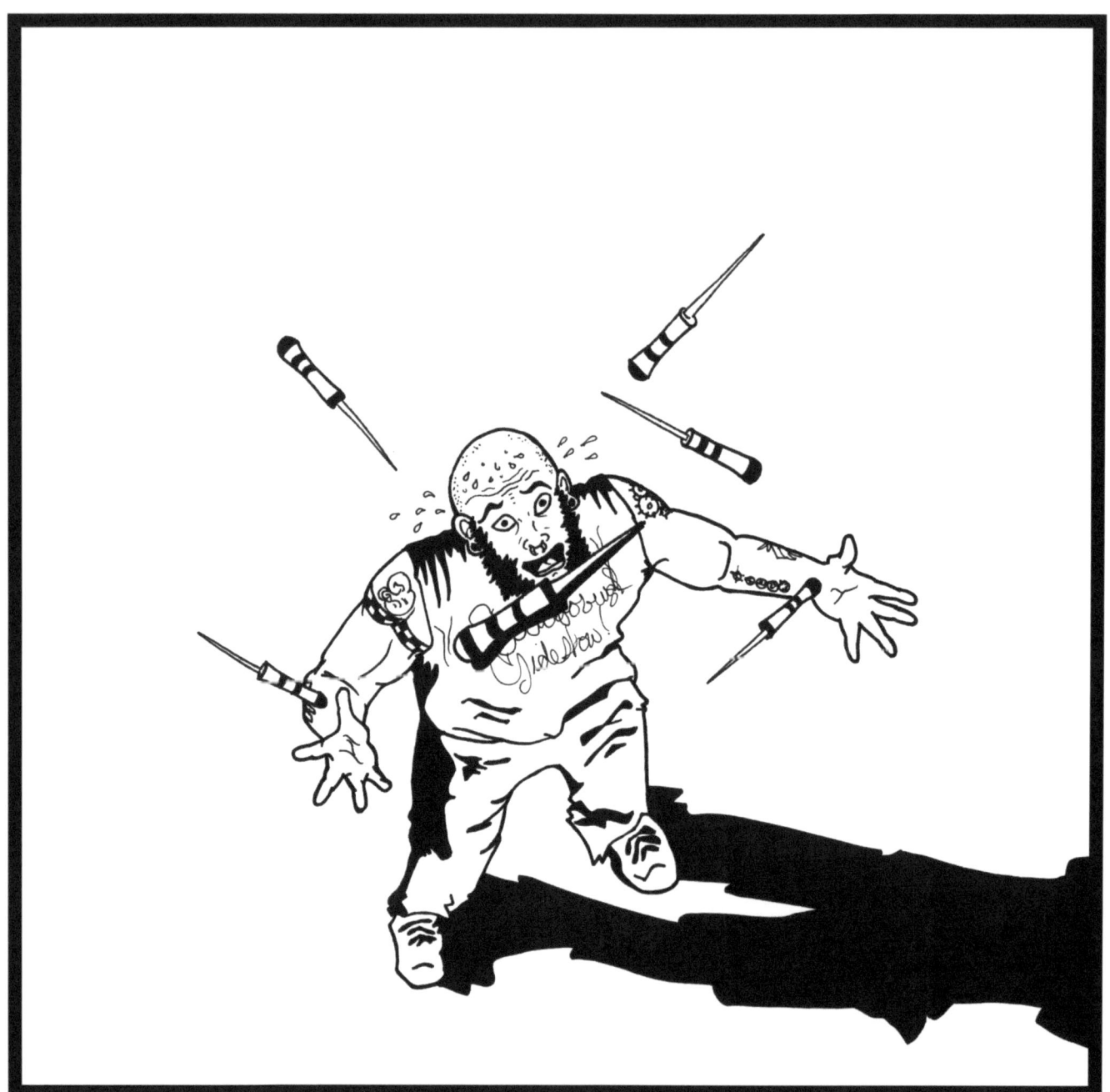

ICEPICK JUGGLING

If hacky sack is too wimpy for you why not try this new X-treme sport? You can always spot veteran icepick jugglers because of their large-gage piercings. The coolest piercing is aortal, but you never get the chance to show it off.

JAWBREAKER

Chipped teeth and torn gums, windpipe plugged by a candy-ball lodged between the last attempt of in-halation and the last sweet taste of sugar dependency.

KNIFE THROWING TRICK

Some prostitutes discover all too late that their customers are into unusual knife play, ala William Tell.

LACTOSE INTOLERANCE

A furious force of chocolate and raspberry jam colored speckles accompanied by tender, blood-coated anus tissue calls for serious forethought upon consumption of dairy.

MASSHYSTERIAMASSHYSTERIAMASSI
STERIAMASSHYSTERIAMASSHYSTERI
RIAMASSHYSTERIAMASSHYSTERIAM
SSHYSTERIAMASSHYSTERIAMASSHY
RIAMASSHYSTERIAMASSHYSTERIAM
MASSHYSTERIAMASSHYSTERIAMASSI
ERIAMASSHYSTERIAMASSHYSTERIAM
SHYSTERIAMASSHYSTERIAMASSHYS
TERIAMASSHYSTERIAMASSHYSTERIA
SHYSTERIAMASSHYSTERIAMASSHYS
STERIAMASSHYSTERIAMASSHYSTERI
ASSHYSTERIAMASSHYSTERIAMASSHY
MASSHYSTERIAMASSHYSTERIAMASSI
SSHYSTERIAMASSHYSTERIAMASSHY
MASSHYSTERIAMASSHYSTERIAMASSI
ERIAMASSHYSTERIAMASSHYSTERIAI
RIAMASSHYSTERIAMASSHYSTERIAM
SSHYSTERIAMASSHYSTERIAMASSHY
STERIAMASSHYSTERIAMASSHYSTER
MASSHYSTERIAMASSHYSTERIAMASS

MASS HYSTERIA

If everybody gets it in their collective head that you're dead you might as well be. Hey, it beats being trampled by parents desperate for the hottest toy of the Christmas season, or falling victim to a witch-hunt.

NUCLEAR HOLOCAUST

Gray ash winters of starvation and mass genocide will put an end to ethnocentric mindsets, dictatorship, and a fascination with testicle related accidents of unknown origins.

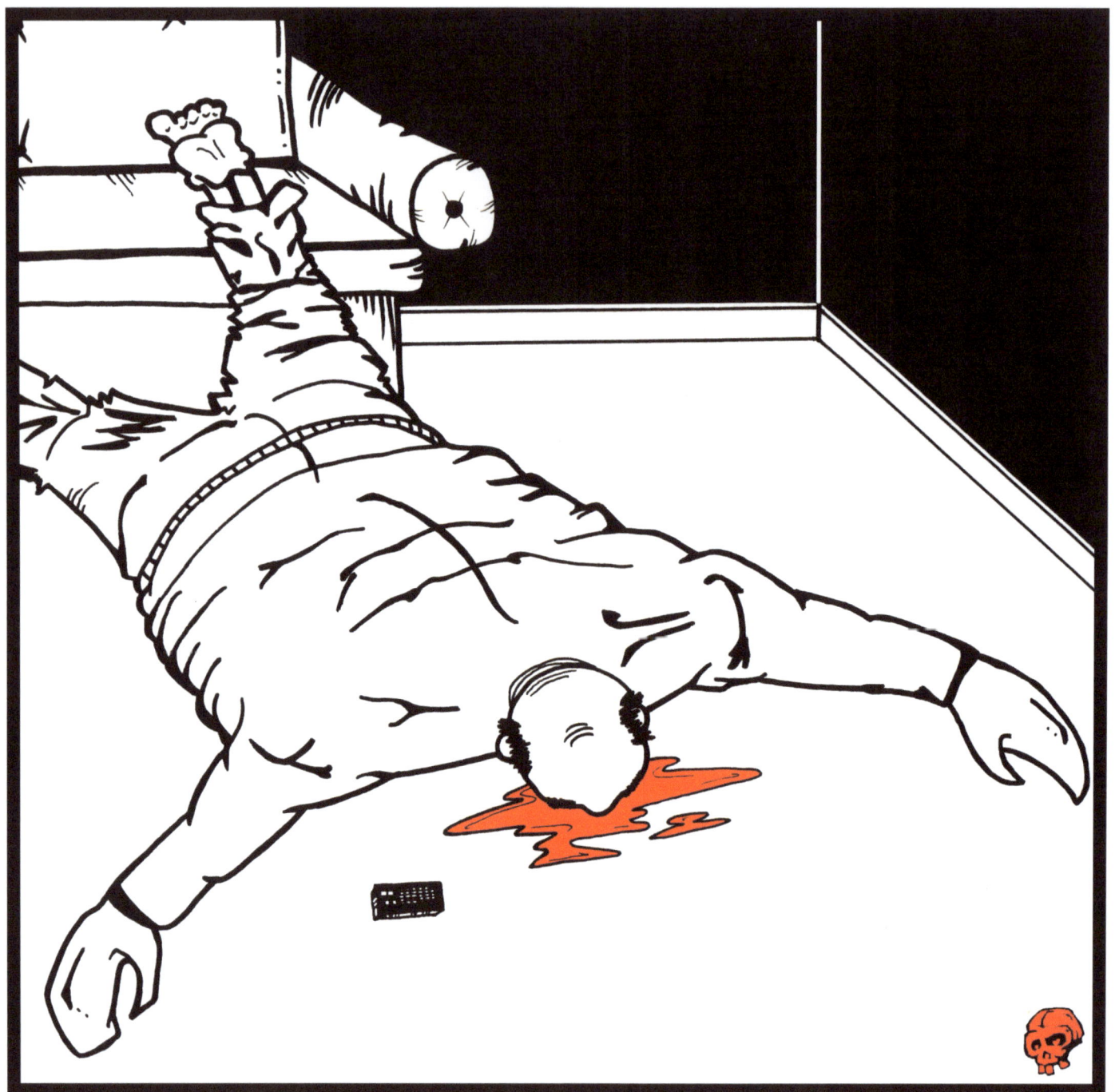

OBESITY

You reach for the remote control and topple from your six-year perch on the sofa. On hitting the floor your obscene weight forces ribs through heart, lungs, and stomach. Would it have killed you to exercise?

PROSTATE DISEASE

The prostate is one part of the male reproductive system where engorgement isn't sought. Don't procrastinate; such could end in your demise. Besides, the exam is only painful when the finger is *inside* your rectum.

QUICK-DRYING CEMENT

You would be surprised how many people use this to patch over holes in their lives. If your friend has a lot of missing ex-lovers you might want to check for new construction next time you stop by.

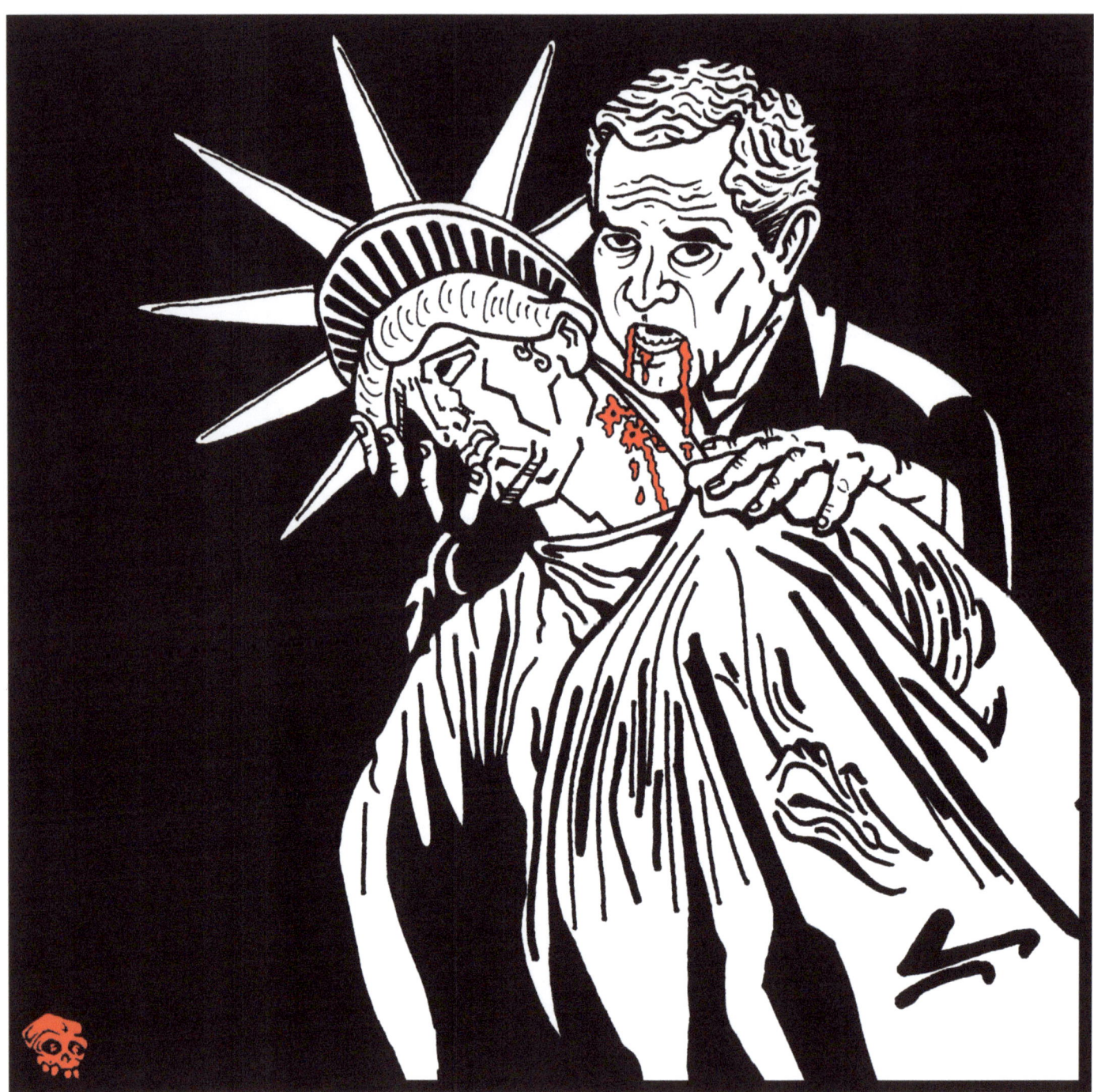

REPUBLICANS

With razor-tongues and words made of bullets, these ignorant minded carnivores are the most dangerous animals on the planet.

SUICIDE

They say suicide is a selfish act, but if there's anything that's all about you it's how you die.

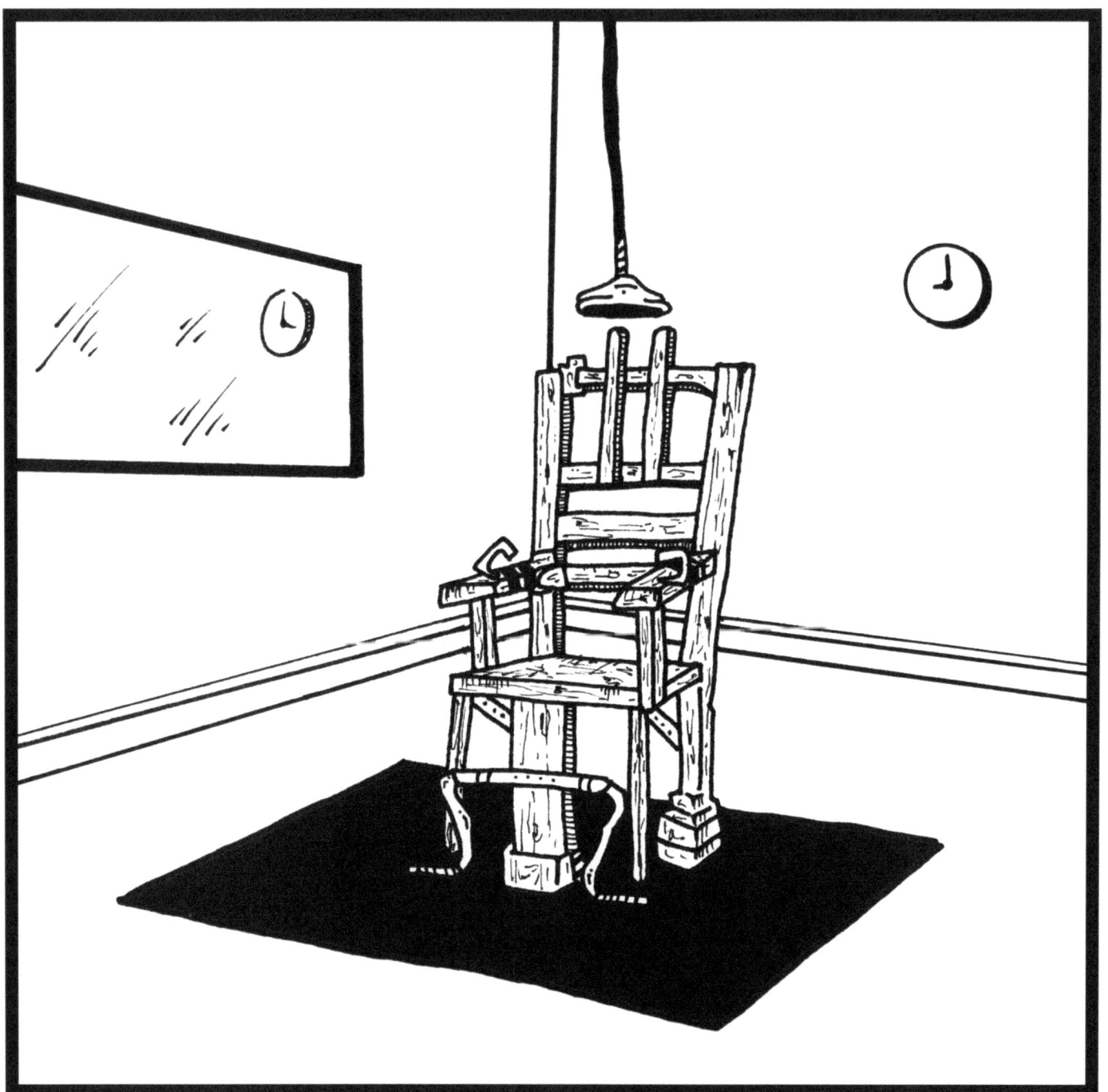

 **EXANS**

They say everything is bigger in Texas, especially the number of state executions.

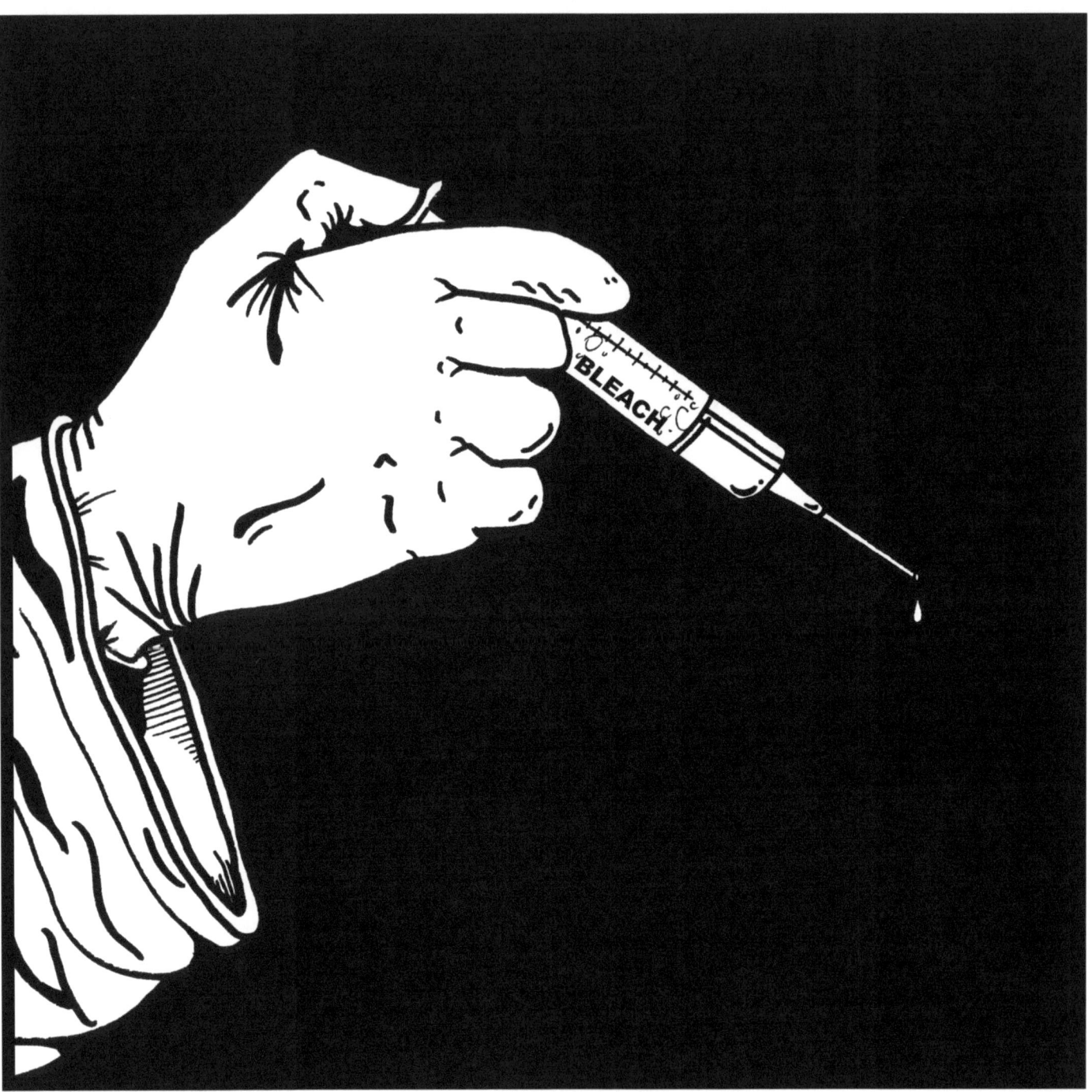

UNETHICAL MEDICAL PRACTICE

If your dentist insists that shooting up bleach will whiten your teeth, maybe it's time for a second opinion. A medical license doesn't make somebody God, and not everyone hangs authentic licenses.

ULTURES

Polly, want a carcass?

WASHING MACHINE HIDE-AND-SEEK

It's better to drown in the wash cycle than to linger for days, locked in cramped darkness, dying of thirst.

XENOMENIA

Blood, blood everywhere, blood, blood in my underwear...

Suddenly, Bill the beer-bellied bigot felt sorry for his lifetime of poking fun at the female menstruation cycle.

YELLOW FEVER

A problem in port cities, the final stage of this darling disease involves regurgitating all the organs it has killed. If you want to impress your dinner guests you can tell them that phase is called "vomito negro."

ZOMBIE APOCALYPSE

When the sky is black and the earth is burnt, they will rise from their graves and prey upon the living. Running will get you no where fast, hiding will find you dead, and fighting will only make your flesh salty and tender.

ABOUT THE CREATORS

DUSTIN LAVALLEY

Dustin La Valley is a writer and martial artist from Glens Falls, New York. His work can be seen online, in print and on film. *A Child's Guide to Death* is his most notorious piece of fiction to date.

JOHN EDWARD LAWSON

John Edward Lawson is an author, editor, and publisher living near Washington, DC. He has been subjected to public education, attack dogs (German Shepherd), stabbings, beatings, and even been hit by cars, yet he refuses to die.

MARK SULLIVAN

M.G. Sullivan hails from Glens Falls, New York. He is a musician, artist, and aspiring author.

DARIN MALFI

Darin Malfi is an artist, writer, and musician whose artwork has appeared in various publications, including *Bare Bone*, the bookplates from the novel *The Fall of Never*, and the illustrated *Child's Guide to Death*, as well as his own independent art. An accomplished drummer, musician, and singer/songwriter, he has performed as one half of the thug-rap duo SP Thugz, the group Dr. Punch Jr., and was the drummer for the award-winning, Maryland-based alternative/metal rock bands Nellie Blide and Verbum Sap. His chapbook, *Wordz of Wizdom*, contains some of his most poignant poetry and collected song lyrics—words that are truly not for the faint of heart!—and his artwork and music can be viewed and purchased at www.myspace.com/darinmalfi, or at www.myspace.com/drpunchjr

Fish, Soap, and Bonds, Larry Fondation
hc 978-1-933293-36-3, $24.95, 160p
tpb 978-1-933293-37-0, $13.95, 160p

Fish, Soap and Bonds follows the movements of three homeless persons on the unforgiving streets of Los Angeles. Through their eyes we experience both the depths and heights of humanity: hate and discrimination, sacrifice and redemption. This is the third in Fondation's series of "LA Stories."

The Troublesome Amputee Collected
Poetry by John Edward Lawson
tpb 1-933293-15-2, $8.95, 104p
hc 978-1-933293-24-0, $18.95, 140p

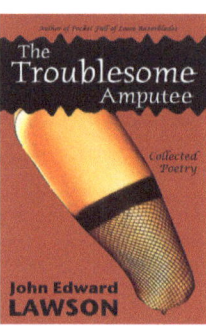

From the introduction by Michael Arnzen: "One of the meatiest collections of grizzly, grotey, bizarro poetry you'll ever come across. The stuff that makes you guffaw with laughter and want to read out loud."

Eyes Everywhere, Matthew Warner
hc 1-933293-18-7, $29.95, 233p

They monitor his e-mails and follow him, they may be reading his mind. Charlie Fields has uncovered a conspiracy of historic proportions. A family friend heads a secret organization bent on controlling the world. Is Charlie crazy, as his wife claims? Or is his family in serious danger?

Meat Puppet Cabaret, Steve Beard
hc 1-933293-16-0, $29.95, 233p
tpb 978-1-933293-31-8, $15.95, 233 p

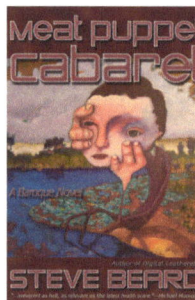

A twisted tale of modern folklore; what if Jack the Ripper were a demon summoned by the black magician John Dee to steal Princess Diana's baby Allegra from the scene of the car crash in Paris? What if Allegra were hidden in a children's home in East London, but then 14 years later escaped?

Vacation, Jeremy C. Shipp
hc 978-1-933293-40-0, $27.95, 160p
tpb 978-1-933293-41-1, $13.95, 160p

It's time for blueblood Bernard Johnson to leave his boring life behind and go on The Vacation, a year-long corporate sponsored odyssey. But instead of seeing the world, Bernard is captured by terrorists, becomes a key figure in secret drug wars, and, worse, doesn't once miss his secure American Dream.

The Million-Year Centipede;
or, Liquid Structures, Eckhard Gerdes
hc 978-1-933293-34-9, $21.95, 130p
tpb 978-1-933293-35-6, $11.95, 130p

Wakelin, frontman of seminal rock group 'The Hinge,' once wrote a poem so prophetic that to ignore its wisdom is to doom yourself to drown in blood. After realizing the power of his words he faked his own death. Now one obsessed fan is tracking Waklin down. Can he be found before it's too late?

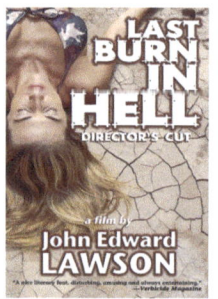

Last Burn in Hell, John Edward Lawson
hc 978-1-933293-25-7, $21.95, 260p
tpb 978-1-933293-26-4, $15.95, 260p

Meet Kenrick Brimley, the state prison's official gigolo. From his romance with serial arsonist Leena Manasseh to his lurid angst-affair with a lesbian music diva, the one constant truth is; he's got no clue what he's doing.

OTHER DARK AND BIZARRE SELECTIONS FROM RAW DOG SCREAMING PRESS

Pseudo-City, D. Harlan Wilson
hc 1-933293-10-1, $29.95, 220p
tpb 1-933293-02-0, $15.95, 220p

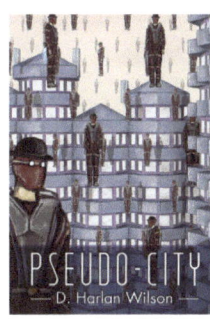

Absurd and surreal *Pseudo-City* exposes what waits in the bathroom stall, under the manhole cover and in the corporate boardroom, all in a way that can only be described as mind-bogglingly irreal.

Fugue XXIX, Forrest Aguirre
hc 1-933293-07-1, $29.95, 220p
tpb 1-933293-12-8, $15.95, 220p

These tales come to you from the fringe of speculative literary fiction where innovative minds keep busy dreaming up the future's uncharted territories and mining forgotten treasures of the past. Anything can happen, and does, with regularity.

And Your Point is? Steve Aylett
hc 978-1-933293-28-8, $19.95, 112p
tpb 978-1-933293-17-2, $10.95, 112p

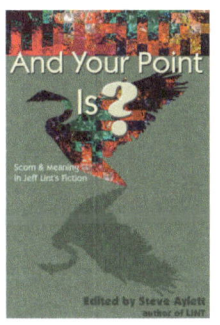

This follow-up to *Lint*, the biography of cult author Jeff Lint, delves deeper into the psychosis of the seminal writer's work. This series of essays and reviews from around the globe, representing decades of study, is being presented for the first time in collected form. A must have for collectors, students, imitators, and stalkers alike.

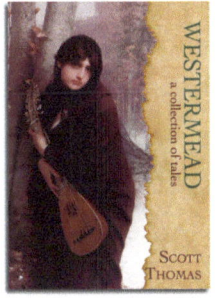

Westermead, Scott Thomas
hc 1-933293-06-3, $30.95, 292p
tpb 1-933293-08-X, $16.95, 292p

Experience Westermead's awakening season by season, the lush heat of summer's passion and the retreat into winter's desolate embrace. Come celebrate and mourn with the people of Westermead as they make their way through a world steeped in beauty and dread.

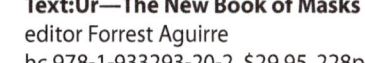

Text:Ur—The New Book of Masks
editor Forrest Aguirre
hc 978-1-933293-20-2, $29.95, 228p
tpb 978-1-933293-39-4, $15.95, 228p

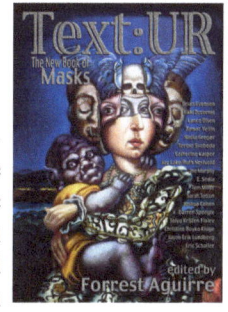

A beautifully surreal masquerade. Fantastical fiction from the most imaginative minds of our time. An hallucinogenic spectacle of literary experimentalism brought to you by a World Fantasy Award Winning editor. Includes fiction by Brian Evenson, Rikki Ducornet, Jay Lake & Lance Olsen.

Sick: An Anthology of Illness
editor John Edward Lawson
tpb 0-9745031-1-8, $15.95, 296p

Collected fiction from authors of horror, surrealism, & science fiction. Here the pen is not merely mightier than the sword; it is a plague heralding the apocalypse for convention. These *Sick* stories are horrendous, hilarious dissections of creative minds on the scalpel's edge.

Tempting Disaster editor John Edward Lawson, tpb 1-933293-00-4, $15.95, 260p

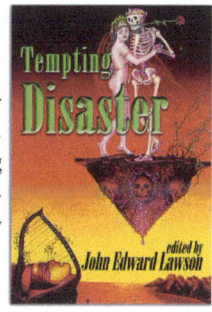

An anthology from the fringe that examines our culture's obsession with taboos. By turns humorous and horrific, shocking and alluring, these authors dissect human desire and those impulses we deny ourselves on a daily basis.

Dr. Identity, D. Harlan Wilson
hc 978-1-933293-23-3, $29.95, 208p
tpb 978-1-933293-32-5, $14.95, 208p

Follow the Dystopian Duo (Professor Blah Blah Blah and his doppelgänger) on a killing spree of epic proportions through the irreal postcapitalist city of Bliptown where time ticks sideways, artificial Bug-Eyed Monsters punish citizens for consumer-capitalist lethargy, and ultraviolence is as essential as a daily multivitamin.